The ship lurched again and the deck tilted. The copper picked up speed, slid sideways . . . and crashed violently into the rail. The rails cracked and splintered under the weight, and the whole thing hung for a moment, right on the edge of the deck. Then there was another jolt. It caught the sun. It flashed red-golden light at me, tilted over the edge . . . and dropped.

THE COPPER TREASURE

MELVIN BURGESS

ILLUSTRATIONS BY

RICHARD WILLIAMS

📚HarperTrophy®
An Imprint of HarperCollins*Publishers*

Library of Congress Cataloging-in-Publication Data
Burgess, Melvin.
  The copper treasure / Melvin Burgess ; illustrations by Richard Williams.
   p.   cm.
  Reprint. Originally published: New York : H. Holt, 1998.
  Summary: In mid-nineteenth century London, three young boys try to retrieve a
valuable roll of copper from the bottom of the Thames River.
  ISBN 0-380-73325-0 (pbk.)
  [1. Buried treasure—Fiction. 2. Friendship—Fiction. 3. Adventure and adventur-
ers—Fiction.   4. Thames River (England)—Fiction.   5. London (England)—
History—1800–1950—Fiction. 6. Great Britain—History—19th century—Fiction.]
I. Williams, Richard, 1950– ill. II. Title.
PZ7.B9166 Co 2002   2001039821
[Fic]—dc21   CIP
                                                                      AC

THIS BOOK IS FOR THE BEAUTIFUL JUDITH.

WITH THANKS TO JEREMY MULDOWNEY

AND JOHN CLARE.

Contents

THE COPPER
TREASURE

ONE
The Tall Ship

Ten Tons made it up first. He landed on the deck with a thump and started bawling and swaggering about like he does.

"Come on up, my little rats! I'll pickle yer livers and slice yer souls! This is the Admirable half-Nelson Ten Tons . . ."

He never got any further because Patty landed and clouted him round the face with a wet sack. Ten Tons screamed, Patty lashed out again, hard. She was a mean old cow, Patty. She was old enough to be your grandmother, and as mean as a rat.

Davies slid over the rail and took her by the arm.

"Leave him," he said.

"Him and his great gob," she hissed. "He'll have the whole dock on us." Then she winced and pulled away where he had her arm. Davies was digging his fingers in hard so it hurt. He waited a few seconds, giving her a long look while she tugged at his stiff fingers. Then he let her shake herself free.

Davies was a stick of a boy. You'd have thought Patty was big enough not to take that from him, but he was hard. You only had to look at him to know he'd do anything.

"You deal with him then, Captain," she sneered, and she flounced off.

It was 1850-who-knows-what, and the whole of the Thames from one end of London to the other was hard at work. There were tugs thumping up and down, pumping out black smoke. There were sprities with their muddy red sails nipping in and out. There were men shouting and whistling, and the rattle of rope and the flap of the sails, and the whole dock was swaying with masts. We were on board a tall ship. She'd have sailed to America and back, that ship . . . she'd have gone round the world and thought nothing of it. She was as big as a cathedral, as high as Heaven, and we were on board thieving.

Ten Tons had his courage back with Davies next to him. He was strutting up and down flicking his suspenders like he owned the whole river. "Give that woman a taste of the lash, Mr. Davies!" he yelled. "I'll have no duck-bummed Paddy-woman poisoning the air on my ship!"

Patty ignored it and went below decks. Tens was always going on like that. If he hadn't been friends with me and Davies I reckon he'd've been killed years ago.

Mind you, she was right. The last thing you wanted was Tens raving away on a job like this. But he was one of us . . . us three. We were in it together. If Patty wanted to come thieving with me and Davies, she had to go thieving with Ten Tons, too. That's just how it was.

He was strutting up and down saluting and grinning. The deck was so high we didn't have to hide, no one could see us. A tug paddled past. I heard its whistle go and a thick clot of black smoke drifted over us. I sniffed the air . . . I love the smell of coal smoke. Then a cloud moved in the sky and the sun shone. Along the deck there was a glorious flash of soft red light.

That's when we first saw it. The treasure, I mean.

It was a huge gleaming roll of brand-new copper. I never saw so much copper . . . it was enough to cover the whole hull! It was all rolled up there on deck right by us. It blazed at us. It was beautiful.

Copper! Ten Tons recovered first. "My love," he cried. He flung himself at it and started kissing it.

It was something, that copper. Like a huge roll of new money. Copper's the best thing you can find on the river. We go to the shipyards every day to see if any's been dropped over the side, but we don't get it very often.

Ten Tons was heaving at it as if he could put it in his pocket. We laughed! Ten men couldn't have budged it. It was worth a fortune! He shouted with pleasure. Then he started dancing about and leering at his reflection in it. He never stayed still for a second.

"Your Highness," he crooned. "Your Copperiness. The Duchess Ten Tons, at your pleasure."

Davies licked his lips and looked at the copper greedily. It was there for the taking . . . except how did you pick up half a ton of copper? If it was pure gold we'd have had to leave it there.

"Come on, Tens," he said. "Let's get going."

We started picking our way across the decks looking for bits and pieces but there wasn't much so we followed Patty below and started going through the cabins for spoons and knives and stuff.

Ten Tons was going on the whole time. I could hear him two cabins away. "A fine collection of cutlery here, boys, we'll eat like kings tonight, o ho," he cackled in a Scots accent. He was always putting on voices. He only had to listen for a second and he got it just right. Oh, he was a treasure all his own, Ten Tons was . . . there was a whole crowd of 'em in that one!

"Come on, Tens," called Davies from the corridor.

"Aye, General," shouted Ten Tons, and he marched out of the cabin like a clockwork toy, going, "Chicky chocky chicky chocky chicky chocky chock chick chick!"

Patty appeared at the end of the corridor. She was doing well enough, you could hear things rattling away under her skirts. She rolled her eyes at me, but I didn't roll mine back. Ten Tons was a madman, but he was our madman.

I was mad myself, thieving like this. It wasn't worth my while. Davies and Ten Tons were orphans, they had to get by how ever they could. But I'd got a mother and father and a proper home. I didn't need to do this. The others were all teasing me because I kept popping up and down above decks to check that it was all clear, but it was just as well I did.

I poked my head up and . . . and there was the dock floating past.

I thought . . . what? Someone was herding cows on the bank . . . we'd drifted right across the river. He pointed at us and shouted. The ship dipped and began to circle and I realized . . . Damn!

She was adrift. The anchor had come loose and we were away downstream like a battering ram. "Davies, Tens!" I screamed. "She's away!"

Ten Tons was up on deck like a cork.

"By God, I've stolen a whole ship this time!" he yelled. He stuck his chest out and started marching up and down the decks giving orders to no one. It was so funny! He's only about a yard tall and he was going up and down the deck like a mad little engine. Davies was up as well, leaning over the side by the rope we'd used to swarm up on board.

"We better get . . ." began Davies.

Then the whole thing lurched.

We'd hit. We'd floated sideways across the river straight into a tug. The ship shuddered. Everyone was flung to the deck. Davies only just stopped himself from going overboard. I saw Ten Tons sliding along on his bum going, "Whhhhhooooah!" I managed to grab hold of the rail. And then the air was filled with a strange, wobbling music. I'd never heard anything like it. I looked along the deck and saw . . .

The copper! What a sight! The bands had broken and it was rolling along the deck, opening itself up into a sheet of shining red. It was like watching a magician spread open his cloak. The ship lurched again and the deck tilted. The copper picked up speed, slid sideways . . . and crashed violently into the rail. The rails cracked and splintered under the weight, and the whole thing hung for a moment, right on the edge of the deck. Then there was another jolt. It caught the sun. It flashed red-golden light at me, tilted over the edge . . . and dropped.

I watched it go down. It hummed as it fell. It flashed in the setting sun and sent a beam of red light across the river. Then it hit the water. It was so bright it looked red hot, I almost expected it to hiss. There was the most almighty splash and a deep gulp as the water swallowed it . . . and it was gone. Half a ton or more of brand-new copper, gone down below and lost forever.

The ship was sluicing sideways.

"They're coming!" yelled Davies. He'd climbed a bit of the way up the rigging, and he could see boatloads of men rowing out to secure the ship. "Run, boys!"

But Ten Tons was staring down at the river where the copper had gone. The water was still and calm. He had a look of ecstasy on his face.

"Sunken treasure," he groaned.

"Come on!" screamed Davies angrily. You can see the danger . . . we'd get the blame for cutting the ship adrift. We ran like rats to the broken mooring rope.

By the time we got there Patty was already on her way down. She let go halfway and hit the water with a huge splash and sank like a stone. The old witch had been to the kitchens and had half a ton of saucepans tied up under her skirts. Davies didn't bother with the rope; the men were coming up the sides already. He jumped. Ten Tons jumped after him. I didn't have the nerve and started down the rope, but the men were leaning over the side by now. There was no choice. I screamed and let go and fell . . .

And fell and fell and fell and fell and fell and fell and fell . . .

I hit the water like a brick. I was under for ages. I came up gasping and spluttering and struck out for the shore. I was ten strokes on when Patty rose up next to me. She must have been under for a minute. She was desperate . . . gasping and thrashing for air. She struck out to grab hold of me, but I kicked her off . . . she was twice as big as me, she'd have pulled me under. I looked back a minute later and she'd got her breath back. She was furious because she'd had to cut the saucepans loose. She wriggled out of her dress, spitting and hissing like a horrible old cat and screaming at me for leaving her. I swam like fury and she wasn't far behind.

TWO
The Dreams

Don't get me wrong. I don't live by stealing. I'm a worker. I have responsibilities. If my father or mother found out I'd been on that boat they'd skin my back with the belt.

One day, they'll skin my back once too often and I won't come back and then they'll be sorry. Davies and Ten Tons are always on at me to go and live with them and let my family look after themselves. They say, "They take your money and spend it on milk for the baby and a new dress for your sister." To tell the truth, I'd like to be my own man, but . . . they're my parents! They brought me up.

There are good things in a family, anyway. That day we got aboard the tall ship, Davies and Ten Tons went back dripping wet to sleep in an old barge half sunk in the mud by Bow Creek. My mother had dry clothes for me and there was a fire even though it was April. When Davies broke his jaw, he lay in that wet barge for three weeks on his own with only Ten Tons to look out for him. If I get ill my mother buys medicine for me, and I get thick broth to eat every day.

When I tell them that, Tens' eyes go as round as hoops. He can never hear enough about having a family. But Davies is harder.

"A man has to make his own life. You'll come and live with us one day, won't you, Jamie? And we'll get ourselves a berth on a boat and see the world."

"Yes, yes!" cries Ten Tons.

"One day," I say.

Oh . . . I'd leave home tomorrow if I could do that. The thought of sailing away down the river and out to sea . . . it makes me ache to think about it, I want it so much. It's all we three ever dream about.

We don't want to be a coalwhipper like my dad, unloading coal from the brigs that come down from the north. We're going to sail round the world and see all the places and people we rule over, and the savages, who have to do whatever a British boy tells them. Even the poorest lad can see the world if he lives on the river . . . except someone like Ten Tons, who's not good for much. But we'll look after him, me and Davies. He says he's going to dress up in feathers and pass himself off as a parrot. He's clever, Ten Tons, but what good's brains if you're small and weak? He's lucky he's got us!

Us three! Right round the world and back! Except . . .

Except it's not so easy. If you're a man it's one thing, but us boys . . . we'd have to buy our way on board ship to learn a trade. I don't want to wait until I'm a man, but I had as much chance of saving up to buy my passage as Ten Tons did of being a parrot. If I ever do make any spare money, my family just gobbles it all up.

It's not fair. It's not my fault my father and mother have more children than pennies. But even if I did leave home I still couldn't get a berth. If it was so easy to earn all that, do you think Tens and Davies would still be here? I once spoke to a cabin boy and his father paid five pounds. Five pounds! I thought you could buy a whole ship for that money.

Come to think about it . . . maybe Ten Tons' idea of disguising himself as a parrot is better after all.

There's eight of us in our family. We live in a couple of rooms on Burcham Street. There's my mother and father and me and Ellen, who's six, and David, who's eight, and Joan, who's . . . well, I forget how old Joan is, except she's not so big as me. Then there's Sally, who's only very little, and the oldest, Mary. Mother and Father are always on at her to move out. That's not counting the baby. Mother said she didn't know where it came from, since she thinks she's too old for them now. But he's sickly and no one expects him to live. Mother says it'll be a relief when he dies. The poor little thing suffers too much and anyway, he cries all night and it makes our lives harder.

I'm eleven years old and I'm four and a half feet high. Davies and Ten Tons don't even know how tall they are, but I'm taller than either of them even though I'm the youngest of us three. I went to school for three years, and I know my alphabet. I can read, but I'm not much good at writing. I used

to go to school with Mrs. Prenderghast. My dad paid
her with a little bag of coal every week. Davies don't
know *a* from *b* but Ten Tons can read and write and
count up to a hundred. He taught himself. He's the
cleverest person I know.

I love my mother and father and I'm proud to be
a working man and help keep us all fed, but the
trouble with honesty is, you have to work hard and
get nowhere. As they say . . . light fingers make light
work. It's nice to feel proud, but I often think I'd
rather be a bit more ashamed of myself and have a
life living with Ten Tons and Davies.

THREE
The Plan

Low tide was early next morning.

I'm a mudlark. I make my money by picking up the coal that falls out when they're unloading the brigs. I have a little basket strapped to my back. Sometimes I fill it twice in a day. Not that often, though.

I'm a good worker. I go out mudlarking even in the winter when most of the others can't stand the cold. It was only me and Davies and Ten Tons and maybe Patty and a couple of others by Blackwall pier this winter. Ten Tons and me are fine with it, but Davies turns blue with cold. I'm tougher than Davies, even though he's stronger than me. I can work all day even in the winter, when you have to crack the ice to lever the coals out of the mud. It's all

Davies can do to sit on the bank and shiver and cry because his hands and feet hurt so much.

Sometimes the coal lies on the surface of the mud, but often it sinks under. Then you have to feel in the thick mud with your toes and hands. It's exciting when you find a big piece, but it's usually little nibs. When the basket's full I take it and sell my coal to the old women up and down Cotton Street or around All Saint's.

We don't just pick up coals, we pick up anything that gets dropped, just about. You get a farthing a pound for old iron. You get ha'pence for bits of rope. If you find fat the cooks have dropped overboard you can get three farthings for that. For good new copper, you can get up to four pence a pound.

Most things can be sold in this world. Once I made a shilling in a day. Mostly it's more like seven or eight pence.

The boat we'd been on yesterday was back at her mooring. She was a merchant ship in for re-rigging. That tug had holed her above the water line, so they'd have to tow her down to a yard to fix it. They use copper to line the hull to keep out the worms in the hot South Seas. Every now and then they drop some into the water, and the workmen don't bother going down to fetch little bits . . . so maybe we'd get some copper off her after all.

There was no sign of that big roll, though. They had men by the dozen floating around trying to spot it, but the water was muddy and deep. They had no chance. Only the fish knew where that was . . . and what good was it to them?

Me and Davies and Ten Tons were treading in the mud around the brigs but I tell you, that copper was driving the three of us mad. The thought of it just lying there glorious and shiny in the ooze . . . there for the taking!

If you could sell that to the marine-store dealer you'd be rich. Even Ten Tons could buy a berth aboard ship with that. All you had to do was pick it up and walk away with it. . . .

I think all three of us'd been thinking about it the whole time, ever since it went down. It was so near! But of course it was just a dream. That copper was sunk too deep to ever fish up again. It was down there along with all the other precious things that have been swallowed up by Old Father Thames over the hundreds and hundreds of years. Even the rich people couldn't have it back now.

Ten Tons stared across the choppy brown water. "It's out there waiting," he groaned.

"It'll have a long wait," I said.

Ten Tons looked up at me and winked. "Waiting for me to get some sense into my head," he said. Then he started doing a stupid dance in the mud. It was too early for jokes. I turned away, treading for coals. The mud sucked at my feet. It was cold deep down there.

"I swam down to it this morning," said Ten Tons suddenly. "It took me thirty dives."

"Did you?" That was something! See? People think Ten Tons is just a madman. But he can stick with things like no one once he gets going. I told you he taught himself to read and write. The trouble is, most of the time he sticks with stupid things . . . well, what does he need to read for? Come to that, what did he need to know where the copper was for? No one was ever going to lift THAT out of the mud, that was for sure.

"It's about two fathoms down at low tide. Down there . . ." He pointed at the place on the water and I could just picture it shining like an angel under the river . . . yes!

"Do you think we could saw bits off?" I asked hopefully.

"Naw!" He looked sideways up at me and he said, "I've been having a think about it, Jamie-boy . . ."

Then Davies saw us talking and shouted, "Get on with it!" Him and Ten Tons worked together. You only get a few hours to get in your coals and bits of iron. Davies would thrash him if he thought he was slacking.

Ten Tons hefted his basket onto his shoulders and shouted, "I must have ten tons of coal in here, Davies!" He always says that. Davies swore and ran his arm along his nose. Green snot. Davies always had green snot running out of him, even in the summer. He said it gave him a headache. Maybe that's why he gets so cross.

We ate our grub on the jetty. I had a chunk of bread with dripping on, but all Davies and Ten Tons had were stale crusts. I was going to tell them what I had for supper last night for a tease. I used to say neither of them would know supper if it got up and hit them. But Davies was sitting there holding his face and staring over the brown water, and I kept my mouth shut. You keep quiet when he's like that.

All the time Ten Tons kept glancing at Davies and giggling. You could tell he had something on his mind and I was willing to bet I knew what it was.

The copper.

That's Ten Tons! He's always coming up with these crazy schemes to get rich. And of course none of them ever worked. Well . . . if they had we'd have been rich men by now, wouldn't we?

After eating I went to sell my basket of coal. I found an old woman soon enough on Cotton Street, who gave me three farthings for it. It began to rain, but, well . . . that doesn't bother me! I'm wet all day, I don't even notice it. I had the weight of that coal off my shoulders, that was all I cared about.

The tide was in by now, the coals all covered up, so I went onto the river to collect sticks for my mother to burn. I found a row boat on the jetty . . . no one minds you borrowing the boats, they always get put back . . . and I pushed out into the traffic.

The river's always busy. There was a tug pounding up the river, gushing thick black smoke from its funnel, paddles spinning. You'd think they'd knock a hole in themselves, with their engines thumping away like that. There were the tall ships that cross the oceans, floating on the water with their fine sails like grand ladies. I thought, one day I'll be a sailor and ride all day on one of those.

There were ferry boats carrying people to and fro, the fishermen flinging out their nets. There were the Thames barges and schooners and ketches. There was traffic everywhere. The river was yellow-brown with mud. I was a part of it.

I found a long stick to reach over the side with, and I started fishing for wood.

I always stored my wood in the barge Tens and Davies lived in until it was time to go home. The barge was half rotted, sunk on its side in the mud, and close enough to the docks for us to keep an eye on it as we worked, but even so people used to come and try and steal our stuff. Then we'd have to run back through the thick mud, falling and slipping and black with ooze, while the thieves tried to run back up to the banks. It was the slowest chase you ever saw!

Davies and Tens lost a lot of wood that way . . . it was dangerous in the winter. A lot of orphans froze to death as they slept for the want of a fire.

I could hear Ten Tons snivelling as I got close. I leaned over and dumped my wood through a hole in the hull. Tens was sitting inside. The side of his face was a fiery red. Davies was nowhere to be seen.

Ten Tons sniffed and wiped his face on his sleeve as I climbed in. I went over to him and had a look. It looked really sore.

"He just kept on slapping me," moaned poor old Tens. Davies shouldn't loose his temper on Tens like that. He gets carried away sometimes.

I winked at Tens. "Never mind, Tens. He'll be sorry . . . he always is. Come on. Let's get to work."

I took Ten Tons by the hand and we walked together out of the hulk and onto the mud.

There was a brig beached on the mud, and as soon as we got behind it Ten Tons wiped his face on his sleeve, which made it dirtier than ever. Then he said, "I'll show you instead."

I sighed and leaned against the hull.

He took a short rod of iron and some lengths of string out of his coat and tied the string around the iron. He looked at me and winked and grinned.

I sighed. The iron was meant to be the copper. What else? That's why Davies had attacked him . . . he was sick to death of another mad plan. But I didn't say anything. I felt sorry for poor Tens so I just watched.

Next he got some pieces of wood and he tied those to the other ends of the string. Then he put the whole thing into a puddle. The iron sank to the bottom, of course, and the wood floated.

"Watch," said Tens. He put his hands flat under the wood. "My hands are the water," he explained. He lifted his hands up a little and looked at me. I nodded . . . I got the picture. His hands rising in the air were the water rising as the tide came in. And the

sticks of wood floating on top of the water were being lifted up by the tide. . . .

Slowly he lifted his hands up . . . up, up, up. The string tightened. Then, very gently, as if he were lifting a baby, Ten Tons lifted the iron clear of the mud so it swung free in the air.

"I am the tide, the iron is the copper," he chanted. "What do you say, Jamie?"

I stared at it, imagining half a ton of copper swinging free of the deep Thames mud, slowly sliding away on the current downriver, buoyed up by the timbers, the whole vast weight of it lifted up by Old Father Thames as lightly as if it were a feather on the air. The copper would be as light as that to the river and the copper was enough to buy all of us any life we wanted. . . .

"Damn you, Ten Tons!" I shouted. "Just let me get going, will you?" And I stamped off into the mud to hunt for lost lumps of coal.

I was furious! God knows how many hours we'd wasted trying to carry out those mad plans of his . . . and they never work! Once he had us for three whole days trying to steal a brass sextant he'd seen shining in the sunlight from the cabin of a clipper. We got caught on board and whipped with tarred rope by one of the hands, like real sailors. Poor old Ten Tons got whipped again once we got off . . . by me and Davies. And I got whipped again as well when my father saw the marks.

Tens always made it sound so likely! And now he was at it again!

Half an hour later I was dragging Ten Tons by the hand to go and see Davies.

He was treading for coals farther downriver. He stood straight and watched us, unsmiling, as we came round to him.

"Davies," I said. "You've got to listen to this one."

"If it's another of his plans . . ."

Ten Tons was hiding behind me. "It only takes one of 'em to work, Davies," he squeaked.

"I've got work to do," he growled, and he turned his back.

"Davies, this is driving me mad. Just listen. Ten minutes. Please," I begged.

Davies' face turned hard as a lump of iron. I could

hear Ten Tons tittering nervously. He always giggles when he gets scared. I gave him a nudge. "Get on with it," I said.

Ten Tons went through the whole rigmarole with the iron and the sticks and the string. Davies watched without saying a word. When it was done he clenched his fists and he hissed, "I'll kill him!"

I grabbed Ten Tons' hand and we ran away, through the mud and downriver to the flour mill.

An hour later Davies suddenly appeared next to us. Me and Ten Tons held our breath.

"Ten Tons," he said. "I'm sorry I hit you."

"That's all right, Davies," said Ten Tons, and he began to cry. He always cries when someone says sorry to him. God knows why.

Davies squatted down on his haunches, his bum in the mud, and explained the rest to us.

"We float it downriver while the tide is high," he said. "Then we cut the ropes. The copper drops to the bottom. We wait for the tide to go back out, come back at night . . . and there it is, boys, lying in the mud waiting for us. We'll have to pinch a pair of horses to drag it out and get it to the dealers. And then, my boys . . . we go to sea! Ten Tons . . . you're a genius!"

He jumped up and grabbed Tens, and he grabbed me . . . and we all did a mud waltz, round and round in circles, rubbing black mud in each other's hair and crowing and kissing Ten Tons, and bouncing him up and down. Because, I tell you . . . who else could have thought of it? Who else but Ten Tons! Didn't I tell you? Didn't I? Didn't I?

FOUR

The Rope

Davies wanted us to go straight away and steal rope. We needed lots of good rope if we were going to float that copper off the bottom. But . . . it was the old problem.

I had money to earn for my family.

I couldn't make them see. They thought if you had a mother and father, all you had to do was open your mouth and the food just fell in.

Davies looked anxiously at me. "You make up your mind, Jamie. It's no use me and Tens doing all the work and then you coming up and saying, 'It's all us three together, and where's my share?' "

Ten Tons stood there with his hands behind his back squidging up and down in the mud. We were all covered from head to foot.

"You know I'll get whipped if I take time off," I whined. "Why can't we just do a few hours each day?"

Davies shook his head.

"You can't have both," said Ten Tons.

Davies put his hand in the middle. Ten Tons put his hand on top of that.

"Are you with us, Jamie?" said Davies.

I thought about my mother sitting at home with her tired face and that baby wailing away day and night. I thought of her breaking up a lump of bread into smaller and smaller pieces to feed the eight of us. I thought of my father coming home black with dust and grinning at me when I handed my money over. "You're a man now, Jamie. There's children here'd go hungry if it weren't for you."

Then I thought about Ten Tons, who needed all the help he could get and how there was no one in the world like him. And Davies, who'd break your nose for not much . . . but he'd die for me and Ten Tons if he had to. And I thought of that copper, lying at the bottom of the river like a band of gold.

I said, "I'm with you." I put my hand on top of

theirs and we all swore we were like one man together.

"In the name of Jesus' blood," said Davies.

"In Jesus' blood," said Ten Tons and me together.

And now it had to work because they were all I had.

I said, "But where will we get all that rope?" Davies and Ten Tons looked at me, then at each other, and just started to laugh.

"You tin-head!" screamed Ten Tons. Davies stretched his arm out over the wide river and said, "Wherever we like."

I'm always making a fool of myself like that.

Thing is, there's rope everywhere. Rope ties the sails to the masts, it ties the masts to the deck, and it ties the ship to the dock. Rope furls and unfurls the sails. It lifts goods on and off ship. You use rope to lash down anything that's not nailed to the decks and you lash a man across the back with it, too. I reckon the world would fall to bits if it wasn't for rope.

Funny thing is . . . I never thought you could just take it. The dealer'll buy scraps you've found in the water, but if you turned up with a good length of rope, he'd just shake his head. He knows it means someone's boat's adrift and it's not worth the trouble.

You can't sell good rope. But we weren't planning on selling it.

We waited for high tide in the middle of the night. It was a dark night with a mist on the water . . . just right for this sort of work. Davies suffers from cold so he got the dry job. He went from mooring to mooring along the piers, unlooping the ropes and throwing them into the water. I swam in between the boats, sawing through the ropes with a knife . . . we'd spent half the morning sharpening it up. Ten Tons swam by me, collecting the ropes up.

One by one, the boats we'd cut adrift were sliding away into the dark river. Me and Tens, we got the giggles and half drowned. Those boats'd be halfway to the sea by morning! We kept pulling faces like the men would when they found their boats gone. They were going to go mad!

In the end we nearly got caught. Davies did, anyway. A man with an oil lamp was coming up the pier. The way he was going, he was going to walk smack

into Davies. Me and Tens could see it coming, but poor old Davies hadn't a clue he was going to get nabbed. It was scary and funny at the same time.

I was on deck on a row boat, where I'd found a rope all neatly coiled they'd not stowed. I could hear Ten Tons sniggering to himself from the water below. The man was getting really close and Davies was still running from mooring to mooring slipping the ropes off. He'd get murdered if they caught him.

He got really close and I couldn't stand it anymore. I yelled out, "There's someone coming!"

Davies looked over his shoulder just as the light reached the water and the man saw him . . .

"Oi!"

. . . and . . . splash! He was in the water and swimming for it. The man yelled out in a Welsh accent . . . "Ere, what you doing?" It was too dark for him to see the little boats wagging their way out into the night, so it was a few seconds before he realized.

"Oh . . . my bow-at! My bow-at!" he hooted in that funny sing-song Welsh voice.

Ten Tons picked it up straight away. "My bow-at! Oh, my poo-wer bow-at!" Ten Tons hooted back at him, in a proper Welsh voice.

I was killing myself. Davies swam up and gasped at Tens to shut up in case he gave us away.

"He won't know me, Davies," said Ten Tons proudly.

We all swam quietly off, dragging half a mile of rope behind us. Back on shore the man was still running up and down, wailing, "My bow-at! I'll get you fer this . . . oh my poo-wer, poo-wer bow-at!"

Ten Tons and me nearly drowned ourselves laughing.

We went back to the barge and buried the ropes in the mud, where no one would ever guess. Ten Tons was right about no one recognizing him, though. The next morning they had hold of poor old Jenkins, the Welsh boy who sleeps under the jetty up there, marching him up and down and everyone taking a swipe at him. We must have let slip a dozen boats that night. All the owners were up there and every one of them wanted to knock poor Jenkins down.

"But I did'n do it, no I did'n!" wailed poor Jenkins, while the Welshman roared back, "Do you think I don't know a Welsh voice when I yere one, you bloody little thief?"

And up and down the river there were boats, stuck aground on the mud, or bumped into the jetties or stuck on the side of the bigger ships. Those were the lucky ones. The rest of them were probably halfway to France by then.

FIVE
The Timber

It could have taken us days to get enough timber to float that copper, but we had good luck. It was like this . . . we found a logjam.

A big old fallen willow tree had been washed down and grounded itself in the mud just opposite the Isle of Dogs, and ten big beams were stuck behind it. We rowed across like racers when we saw. Some loose ponies had got down onto the mud and they were trying to get their noses in between them to have a drink, but the beams kept jostling in the water and nipping their hocks and their noses.

The ponies were getting cross but we were delighted. The beams were enormous, at least two foot square and twenty long. It was enough to float that copper twice over!

We did a dance right there among the ponies. Ten Tons tried to dance a hornpipe but the beams were slippery and he fell in. Me and Davies laughed like dogs. The logjam must have passed by a sewage outlet, and the gaps between the logs were choked with . . . well, you know. Ten Tons came up covered in it. I fell in the mud with laughing! Even Davies was bending over and hooting. Ten Tons was smiling like a silly sheep and did a poo-dance in the water, which made us laugh all the more.

Well, we all got covered in it on the way back. It was all over the beams. There's worse on the roads everywhere. Only twenty yards from where I live there's a huge pool of it where everyone dumps their waste. At least in the river there's water to wash in, and it doesn't often come all stuck together like that.

Getting all that wood back safe was a problem, though. We couldn't do it all in one go. In the end we nailed five timbers together with rope like a long tail, and then nailed the long tail to the row boat. Davies and me took the oars in the row boat and Tens sat behind, getting poo-ed up on a beam.

Those five were still too many. Even with the tide behind us, they kept getting stuck and we ended up cutting two loose. We got the other three back safe, and lashed them to the barge. Then we went back to pick up more . . . but by that time there were men arguing over them. We tried telling them we were there first, but they only laughed at us and chased us away.

But our luck wasn't over. On the way back we picked up the two we'd cut loose. That made five. But then we all had a big argument. We were all starving hungry. Me and Ten Tons wanted to sell one of the timbers to a timber yard, but Davies as usual had to do it the hard way.

"What if four's not enough?" he said. "What then? What then?"

"Then it still won't work, because we couldn't control five even without the copper tied to the bottom," said Ten Tons.

Davies hates backing down, but . . . well, the thing is, he was exhausted. It's funny . . . Ten Tons is as weak as a kitten, and Davies is a tough man. But he gets tired while Ten Tons can go on gibbering and running around all night, if he gets the food. You could almost see Davies fading while we argued. So in the end he just waved a hand and sat down with his head in his hands and let us do what we wanted.

Me and Tens paddled one beam down to the timber yard while Davies guarded the other four. Then we bought beer and hot pies. It was a feast! You see? Our luck had turned. We were rich already! And there was still some money left. I knew how cross Davies was going to be when he thought how he'd given way to us just because he was weak, so I bought him a pipe of tobacco, which he loves but he hardly ever gets.

Davies says he's the only one old enough to smoke. Actually, Ten Tons is the oldest. He just doesn't look it.

Davies was laid out like a limp rasher when we got back, but his eyes lit up when he saw the pipe. Me and Ten Tons sat around him and cut his spuds up and gave him the fattest pie. He was our leader. Even though it sometimes looked like just staying alive was enough effort to kill him off.

When it was all done, me and Davies lay down for a sleep and Tens took the first guard. He didn't need so much sleep as normal folks. He stared at Davies with his big bulgy eyes. "It's all right about the beam, Davies," he said shyly. "You'll see."

Davies just puffed on his pipe and smiled. "Go on, then, Tens . . . tell me all about it."

So we both lay down to sleep while Ten Tons' piping voice went through the plan from start to finish. I didn't hear it all. I fell asleep listening to his voice. The last thing I thought was . . . it was sure this time. Nothing could possibly go wrong.

SIX
The Lift

⚓

Next morning me and Ten Tons were itching to get on with the job, but Davies wouldn't let us. "It's night work," he said. "Unless you want the prize taken from us, that is."

So we had nothing to do but sit it out and guard our timbers, and that was a thing in itself. There were a lot of greedy eyes on our wood, wondering why we weren't off to sell it. Old Patty was on to us as soon as the morning mist lifted. She came squelching across, with her skirts tucked into her drawers and a stupid filthy little bonnet on her head.

"Where are you taking that? You won't get more for it sitting down there on your backsides," she told us.

Ten Tons started giggling but Davies just yawned in her face. "Get lost, Patty," he told her.

"There's four beams, that's one each," she said, sticking her nose in the air as if we'd cheated her. But we weren't about to let her in on this game . . . she wasn't one of us. She started screeching and swearing at us and making out we were cheating her, and we had to pelt her with mud and chase her away.

Then after that there were some men nosing about the bank. Davies got the idea they were getting a few of them together to steal our wood, so we loosed the timbers and set sail on them. No one could catch us out on the water, but it was too hard . . . that wood was heavy! In the end we got a rope and a big stone and made ourselves an anchor, and we spent the rest of the day sitting in the middle of the river, basking, doing nothing.

I was glad we'd left the barge, because at midday my father came down to look for me. My heart was pounding when I saw him! I slid off my log and hid behind it, and Davies and Ten Tons laid low, too.

I watched him cross the mud and go into the hulk and then come out again, casting along the river for signs. He saw the timbers and stared, but he couldn't make us out. Then he turned his back and toiled his way slowly back up to the dock.

I felt ashamed. I made a promise to myself that once the treasure was ours, I'd share half my profits with him. That made me feel better. I began to imagine that I was a fine fellow after all and not the runaway I really was.

As dusk fell we went back to the barge to wait for the tide to go out. We needed the water low when we tied the copper to the timbers, so that the rising tide could lift it.

Everything was right. It was dark, but with a bit of moon so we could see each other. The tide was low at eleven. By two or three in the morning the water would have risen far enough to float the beams and we'd have a few hours to get the copper down to the pasture.

Slowly the water disappeared from the river bed. You could hear the mud hissing as the water drained out of it.

"This is it, boys," said Ten Tons. "Let's get rich."

I could hardly see him in the dark but I heard him spit on his hands and rub them together. He'd quietened right down, Ten Tons had . . . as if the copper had straightened him out.

The first thing was to get the ropes onto the copper.

Ten Tons had taken a rope down to the copper earlier and tied a piece of wood at the other end to mark the spot. All we had to do was pull ourselves down that to reach the copper on the river bed.

Under the water the copper had unraveled further. It was huge! It seemed like the bed of the river was all copper, it was that big. It lay there in the dark with the river mud drifting over it, but it felt to me as if it were glowing and lighting up the nighttime underwater . . . filling the river with wealth.

The ropes went on easier than I thought. There were holes drilled into the copper on one edge . . . I don't know why but they were perfect for us. We tied one end of a rope to Ten Tons' marker plank and the other end round our waists. Then, we pulled ourselves down to the copper. You felt your way along the metal until you found a hole and threaded your rope through. Then, back up to the surface, pulling the new rope after you through the hole. It

was easy enough, except you had to do it all under the murky water in one big breath.

Then you tied the two ends of the rope together to make a loop, nailed the loop to a little bit of wood to keep the rope at the surface, got your breath back . . . and down you went again.

It went so well! Usually all sorts of things go wrong with plans. But the ropes slipped in the holes and purred through behind you as you swam up. There were no tangles . . . it was easy! Even so it took a long time to get on the twelve loops we wanted. Then it was time for the next stage.

We went back up to the barge and pushed the beams down through the mud to the water. They weighed a ton . . . we were cursing ourselves for not leaving them tied to a jetty so we could just float them out, but then they might have been stolen. We had to strain like horses to budge them and we were all covered in mud from head to foot by the time we reached the water.

Once we got a beam afloat we paddled it out to the spot where the copper lay. The water was cold and choppy . . . there was a bit of a wind slapping the waves up. It was hard to believe there was enough copper to buy us a life each under there. We just pulled the rope loops over the timber, banged in another nail to stop it slipping, and went on to the next one. Davies had cut each rope to length, so that the timber would lift the metal evenly. The hardest bit was keeping the timber still in the current long enough to get the ropes on. When we had three ropes on, we went back for the next beam . . . and the next . . . and the next.

It was hard work. With the second beam, we had farther to push . . . the tide was still going out. But by the time we got to the third, the distance was shorter. The tide had turned already. We were all exhausted by that time, but the thought that we might be too late made us work even harder.

One by one we got the beams out onto the river and tied in place. And suddenly . . . it was done. Our job was over. It was the river's turn. We sat still on our timbers and waited for the water to work for us.

It's strange on the river at night, with the smoke and bustle of the day all gone. There was only the creak of timber ships and the wind in the rigging.

The water lapped and slapped against our legs. It was dark and open on all sides. We talked in whispers for a bit, and then fell silent. I think we were all scared it wasn't going to work . . . and scared it would, too.

The wind began to pick up and it got cold. You could hear all our teeth going and we played a daft game, making music with our teeth chatters, until Davies went very quiet and I guessed the cold had got to him. We sat there for hours. Nothing moved, nothing changed. It felt like nothing would ever change again. Then, finally, there came a hard, loud creak right by me, like someone treading on a loose floorboard. It made us all jump.

There was a pause.

A moment later there was another hard creak. And another behind Ten Tons. And another. And then . . . there was a soft little groan right in my ear. I opened my mouth to yell, and it came again. There was a man sitting by me in the darkness, crooning! Sure, there was someone there!

"Jesus bless us!" groaned Davies. Then another noise . . . a long groan, as if someone was in pain.

"It's the drowned men!" cried Davies, and I think he and I would have jumped off and swam for it. But Ten Tons sneered, "You pair of babies, it's the ropes taking up the weight, that's all."

I could have wept with relief because I knew at once he was right. I'd heard those noises in daylight a hundred times before from wet ropes stretching over wood. It was the night that was ghostly after all, not the noise. But it made my hair stand on end to listen to the ropes speaking, even though I knew what it was.

"Feel the ropes!" hissed Davies.

I prodded the ropes under me; they'd gone as hard as iron. They were taking up the weight.

"Yes. Yes!" I hissed. I grinned in the dark, and I bet they did, too. There was another long wait. The next thing we noticed was how the timbers were getting lower in the water. Then, they began to drift together. It went on for maybe half an hour, until they were all jammed tight together.

And then everything went very still.

The water lapped at the timber. It was just like it had been before.

Ten Tons said suddenly, "We're moving."

"We never are," said Davies.

"We are. We're moving. We're moving, boys. We're away!"

The timbers began to turn slowly in the water. Two fathoms down below us, the slab of copper swung free of the mud and twisted slowly in the current. We tilted sideways and began to pick up speed.

We were off . . .

Ten Tons went mad. He'd been as sensible as anyone else while the work was on but now that it was done, he just went mad. He was gibbering, shouting snatches of song and kicking up the water. He was up and jumping and dancing along the beam, whirling about like a top.

Me and Davies whooped and splashed the water with our hands, and dug our heels in as if we were riding horses. Ten Tons started on his famous hornpipe . . . but the timbers were wet and of course he fell in with a loud splash. He didn't care. He was still dancing in the water!

After that Davies tied one of the rope ends round Tens' waist so he wouldn't get lost in the dark if he fell in again. Ten Tons was the sort of lad who'd be falling in the whole time, you could count on that.

Away we went, singing and whooping as we sailed down the good old Thames with our fortunes hung below us, like a clipper from China with its belly full of tea!

SEVEN
The Accident

We were having a good time, but not for long. Somehow, like a gang of idiots, we'd thought the timbers would go nose first downstream like a boat. But no sooner had we got away than the current caught the sail of copper under us. We spun slowly round and there we were, heading sideways down river. We sat looking at each other and smirking when Davies yelled, "Look out! It's a bloody ship!"

You could hardly see it in the dark, but it was coming right at us . . . a bloody great ship, sitting in the water like a mountain right in the way. As it got close we could see the black bulk of it. We all paddled like barmy, trying to get round her, but of course we hit. We all flung ourselves off into the water and then . . .

We were still miles from the bank, with no way of stopping or steering.

"We're going to lose it!" I wailed.

"Shut your mouth and work," roared Davies. He won't have thinking like that once he's got going.

We put our heads down and heaved and splashed in the water, while the copper swung beneath us, dragging us down toward the sea. Ahead of us in the east, the light was brightening fast . . . but bit by bit we were getting closer to the bank . . . whether from our efforts or a chance of the current, I don't know.

If we could just get close enough! All we had to do was cut the ropes and let the copper sink. The river would hide it for us until the next night. Then we could come back with horses and more rope, and we'd have the whole night before us to drag it out and get it to a dealer's.

The bank was getting closer, closer. There were plenty of fields this far out. We were going to make it! We were just arguing if it was right to slip the ropes now or best to wait a few minutes more, when the accident happened.

It began with a crack . . . sudden, hard as gunshot. The next thing I knew I was under water. I struggled up. The light was bright enough by now for me to see the white faces of my friends staring at me. The timber I'd been sitting on lifted its nose out of the water, like a whale.

Davies said, "The rope went." I touched my shoulder and found a patch of skin a foot long stripped off my shoulder. I pulled myself up out of the water and in the same moment another went; then another . . .

CRACK! CRACK! and SHHHHHHHHHHHHH-WAAAK! as they struck the water. There was a puff of wet fibers where the rope split on the beam and a long flash of spray where it lashed the river. Those ropes were deadly. It was the strength of the copper lashing out at us.

Then the timbers started to misbehave.

They were twisting and sinking. It was the uneven weight pulling at them as the ropes snapped. Some of them leaned right up out of the water and then crashed back down with a great splash, like the dolphins you see in the harbor from time to time. I fell into the water again and tried to swim clear. Davies tipped sideways as the timber he was on rose into the air like a horse. I saw Ten Tons staring as his beam dipped down and the water rose around his hips. Then the rope slipped off the beam and Ten Tons went straight off the end of it and down with a hard, quick splash.

For a second it was just waves and water and the timbers rising and falling like giant clubs beating the water. We were bobbing up and down trying to duck out of the way. There was a pause. One last timber that must have been dragged right under by the metal suddenly shot up from the depths, nose first. It went up like a salmon and then fell back down with an almighty splash.

And it was all over.

I was cringing in the water. I'd been right in the middle of it, it was sheer luck I hadn't been hit. Just one blow could have killed a horse. The water heaved and the timbers rolled and yawed. I grabbed hold of one. They were moving in the current, swiftly now that they were free of the weight. Davies was a few yards away, splashing and spitting water and reaching for a beam.

Ten Tons was nowhere to be seen.

The water settled. Me and Davies stared around us waiting for Ten Tons to come back up. I said, "Maybe he got washed downstream."

Davies looked at me and as I watched, his face sort of changed shape and color. I suddenly knew . . .

Tens had that rope tied around his waist. Remember? To keep him safe if he fell in? He was tied good and tight to that rope, and the rope was tied good and tight to the copper. Our treasure lay God knows how many fathoms down, and it had Ten Tons with it.

Davies screamed twice, "Tens! Tens!" Then he slipped off the beam and dived. But we'd drifted on. Tens would be yards upstream. I struck out back to where I thought it was and I dived. We dived and came up, dived and came up, dived and dived and dived. The time was ticking by and all the time Ten Tons was under water.

It was awful. He was there somewhere, we could free him if we could only find him. But the water was murky, you couldn't see. I had this terrible fear that he was under there and he might grab my ankles as I swam past and drown me, too. We dived and dived again and again. It was minutes now. I started looking for the big bubbles when his lungs gave out but I never saw them. We must have been far away from where he was.

We kept going down and coming up and going down even when we knew it was all over, even when we knew he must have run out of breath minutes ago. We didn't want to give up.

At last Davies grabbed hold of some wood floating past. I watched his eyes like panes of shining glass.

"Ten Tons!" he yelled, but his voice cracked and he began to cry. I was shattered. I was exhausted and terrified. I kept thinking of Tens under there reaching out for my legs as I swam past. I set out for the bank. Davies screamed up to me to come back.

I shouted back, "He's dead!" and carried on swimming. Davies was floating away from me. I could hear him crying as I swam.

It wasn't far to the bank. I got out and trudged through a margin of mud out onto the edge of a pasture. I turned back to watch Davies. He was miles away, floating downstream, crying his heart out.

There was no one ever like Ten Tons. He was our friend. We should have looked after him better. I lay down on the mud and I began to cry, too. My voice sounded strange to me and I never wanted to breathe again.

I stayed there for ages. Slowly the light came up. The dawn seemed to make everything colder. I was freezing cold and shaking and shivering. I turned away from the whole thing and headed back upstream on the long walk back.

EIGHT
Ten Tons Marks the Spot

I woke up with sunlight on my face.

I was in the barge. I lay there blinking, listening to the calls of the boatmen and the thumping of the tugs making their way up and down the river. For a moment I thought I must've gone to have a doze in the hulk while the tide was high but then I remembered . . .

Ten Tons was dead.

I got up. I couldn't bear to think about it. I wanted to go home to my mother but what good would that do? To get a whipping? Anyway, I was too ashamed. I walked down to the water at the end of the hulk and splashed my face and had a drink. The tide was in. I went outside to find a boat and pick up sticks to burn.

⌐ ⌐ ⌐

I worked very hard all that day. I wanted to work it all away. I kept expecting Davies to turn up. Every few minutes I'd lift my head to look over to the barge but he never came.

What were we going to do now? I wanted Davies to come so much but he stayed away. It was like I was the only one left alive. I thought how Davies had been the one who tied Tens to the copper in the first place, trying to make him safe. I was scared that maybe now he'd just let the river take him away and dump him in the sea to drown. I wouldn't have minded doing that myself.

Even when the light failed I kept at it, feeling in the mud for dropped coals with my feet. I filled my basket twice. When it was too dark to see anything I picked up my bundle of sticks and went back to sleep in the barge.

It was horrible. We were just children who'd messed with things, and now one of us was dead. Davies didn't come back the next day, or the next. I made up my mind he was dead or gone away and that I'd never see him again. I never felt so alone in all my life.

Next morning my sister Joan turned up.

I slept late and I woke to her voice at the edge of the barge. I almost jumped out of my skin. It was funny . . . I was scared of her although she's smaller than me. It was like my whole family was there in her. She was angry at first because my mother and father and all of them had thought I was dead until someone told them I'd been seen. I just sat shivering while she scolded me. Then I told her, "Ten Tons is dead," and she cried, "Oh, Jamie!" and gave me a hug. I cried in her arms and said I was sorry, and she told me my tears were a man's tears, like my father's when our brother Sam died two years ago.

Joan told me to come home, but I said no . . . not until I'd earned enough to make up for the missing days. Then she got cross again, but she was only pretending. She said they all missed me and they'd welcome me back. I knew it was true, but I said how our father'd whip me, anyway.

She said, "Yes, but only because he loves you," which is what my mother always said. That made us both laugh. Then she said she had to go, so I gave her two pennies to give to Mother, and promised I'd come that evening after work. But I never did.

I worked hard all that day again and was up early the next day. I ate almost nothing, but I still hadn't made up the money. But even so I thought to myself, tonight I'll go home. Sleeping alone in the barge every night, thinking about Ten Tons down in the river with the mud in his mouth and the water inside him . . . I'd had enough of that.

And it was then, of course, when I'd decided to go back home, that Davies turned up.

I saw him come out of the barge and tread through the mud toward me. I went round into the shadows. I wanted to hide . . . I don't know why. It was something to do with what had happened to Ten Tons. It felt like we'd murdered him, somehow. Or maybe I wanted no more trouble. But he followed me, and he put his hand on my shoulder.

It was the same old Davies, with his long crooked jaw, his twisted face, his dirty rags, his lungs squeaking away and his face full of snot. He said, "It's still on, and you're still in with me, Jamie. You gave me your word that we were one man together, in Jesus' blood."

I pushed his hand away. He was mad if he thought I was going to touch that copper again! But he seized me by the arm.

"You're with me," he told me.

"No."

"You gave me your word," he insisted.

"We don't even know where it lies," I said, and I tried to twist away. But Davies held me and grinned and nodded.

"I know where it lies," he said. "Ten Tons showed me."

I shivered right up and down my back then. He really was mad. Ten Tons was dead! But he stood there grinning at me, as if he knew something about dead people that I didn't.

"I tell you, Jamie, he showed me. You know how it is with the drowned men. On the third or fourth day they float to the surface. Well, I knew more or less where we went down. I've spent these last days waiting for him. Yesterday he came back up. See? He was two feet under at low tide, face down, float-

ing with his arms and legs stretched out. He looked like he was flying, Jamie . . . you should have seen him! Flying like a kite. His rope led all the way back down to the copper." He nodded again. "So I know where it is, see."

I could feel my mouth hanging open. I said, "Is he still there?"

"I cut him loose. He's in the sea by now. But I tied a piece of wood to his rope to mark it, and I dived down yesterday. And there it was . . . our copper. I've tied the ropes back on and floated them on planks, same as he did. At low tide we can get the ropes up to the bank and drag it out. Do you see, Jamie? It won't be clear of the water but that doesn't matter. It's by a good field, and there's even horses waiting for us . . . and there's a marine-store dealer only a few hundred yards away."

I just looked at him. Was he mad . . . or would it still work?

"But what about Ten Tons?" I asked.

I could feel his hand trembling on my arm. "Ten Tons is dead, Jamie, we can't do anything for him. But he was working with us in his death. Do you see?

He marked the spot. Do you think he'd wish us to leave that copper there? It's his plan. Jesus, Jamie, don't let him die for nothing. Don't let him die for nothing." Davies stood there looking at me and shaking his head, and I watched his eyes fill with tears.

"And when?" I asked.

"Tonight. Low tide. It's all set."

I thought of the copper lying down there waiting to be pulled out and sold, and how my father would forgive me anything if I came back home with gold tied up in my coat. I thought of the boat that might carry me round the world if I could only pay my way for a while. I thought of Ten Tons tumbling through the water, on his way down to the sea.

Davies was right. Ten Tons was helping us even now, when he was dead . . . showing us the way to the sea. He never gave up. He'd never want us to give up. And so I agreed to go along with it.

NINE
The Copper Treasure

Davies was as proud as anything with himself. "I worked it all out," he kept saying. What he'd done was copy Ten Tons, but he'd done it well. He had ten good strong ropes tied to the copper. He'd even spent his spare time while he waited for Tens to come up making halters for the horses.

We pinched a boat and floated down from Blackwall in the very black of night. Then we had to spend another hour rowing up and down in the dark trying to find the ropes Davies had set up. Once we had them, we took them to the shore, stuck the bits of wood they were tied to into the mud to hold them, and set out to catch the horses. The tide was still on its way out, but the light was already at the edge of the sky. We didn't have long before the world woke up.

I say horses. One of them was an old donkey. The second was okay but the other was a boney old nag that looked too tired to pull grass. The old donkey was the worst. Half the time it was him chasing us. He bit, he kicked, he stamped on your feet. Then we got a rope around his neck, and Davies gave him a few licks with a rope end, and that quieted him down a bit.

We got them roped up to the copper easy enough. Then it was a matter of driving them up the field with the metal behind them. Well, it doesn't take long to talk about.

The nag was useless. He just stood there straining away like a paper bag for all the difference he made. The donkey was even worse. He had his head down and his ears flat, watching us all the time from his yellow eyes. If you grabbed him he bit you. If you let him go for a second he ran away down to the water and stood in the mud. If you looked away he edged sideways for a kick. Oh, he was a vicious brute, that donkey.

At last we struggled a few yards up the bank, with the good horse pulling away well . . . and then the

nag suddenly lay down on the mud and went to sleep. Davies ran to it and the donkey twisted sideways and lashed out with its hooves. It knew how to move if it wanted to. It caught Davies a blow on the thigh and knocked him flying across the mud. He was weeping with pain.

After that, Davies got it into his head that the nag and the donkey were in it together trying to trick us out of our copper. He got the donkey in a corner and flogged it till it cried. It was an awful noise. I told you . . . he gets carried away, Davies, although it was no worse than the donkey deserved. It was used to it, I expect.

We pulled and flogged at first one beast then the other. Inch by inch they dragged the copper from its bed in the mud. We were falling and slipping and the beasts were slipping and furious with us for making them work at night. Inch by inch by inch . . . until at last a great shadow appeared out of the water, dark against the silvery moonlit mud.

We ran to and fro with handfuls of water to splash on it . . . and there it was, under the ooze, as glorious and bright and golden red as the morning sun itself.

Our copper, raised up on land. We stretched out on it and rolled on it, kissed it and rubbed up on it. It was ours!

But it wasn't a celebration. Davies held out his hand. "Here's to Ten Tons," he said. "It's thanks to him."

Then it was back to the struggle . . . slipping, falling, slipping, whipping, slipping, fighting inch by inch . . .

We had it out of the river, out of the mud, across the grass. On the grass it was easier. We were going at a walking pace. We were getting there . . . but the sun was up. There was the gate, there was the road that led back down to a rackety wooden pier and the dealer. . . .

We got to the gate and opened it up. On the road it would be plain sailing. We were almost singing as we drove our beasts out of the gate. The copper followed . . . and then it got stuck.

Would you believe it? The gate was too small.

We stood and stared at it in disbelief. Beaten by a gate? It was impossible.

We found some poles under the hedge and tried

to lever the copper up and over, but it was far too heavy. We were running out of time. There was pale light downriver; dawn. We stared and stared and stared, but there was no way that copper was going through that gate.

"What are we going to do, Davies?" I begged. It was just then we could have done with Ten Tons.

Davies said, "Smash the gate."

I thought, he's mad. There was a brick pillar on each side of that gate. But nothing was stopping Davies. He grabbed hold of a lump of stone and whacked it down on the capstone. A piece broke off.

"Smash the gate to bits!" yelled Davies. I grabbed a brick and I caught the capstone an uppercut and it went flying off. Then we got to work on the bricks, one at a time.

And you know what? It worked! The pillars weren't as solid as they seemed at first, all the mortar was crumbling away. We were there like a pair of madmen, pounding away brick by brick, lump by lump, till our arms ached. Poor old Davies was wheezing away so much I thought he was going to collapse, but we kept at it. It was getting light, and soon enough someone'd come along and steal our prize off us. We got it down to half size, and then quarter size. Then we lashed the animals but it was still no use, so we lumped and banged and pounded again.

The donkey brayed, the horses tossed their heads . . . and at last the whole great roll of the copper grated and clattered over the scattered bricks and started to grind its way out of the field.

We were on!

It was the very last leg. We were pushing our beasts as fast as they could go. They were as exhausted as us now, but we showed them no mercy . . . we were nearly home. The copper made the most awful racket, grinding and rattling on the road, and already there were people gathering to see what was going on. Beggar boys and girls, men on their way to work, a couple of young girls hurrying to get on with the milking or something. Some of them were yelling at us for taking the nags . . . I reckon they worked for the farmer. But they didn't stop us. I reckon it was too much of a sight for them to stop us.

And at last, there it was . . . the marine dealer. We got the copper right up to the gate. The nags stopped and hung their heads, panting and sweating foam, and me and Davies flung ourselves at the wooden gate and we pounded and banged and banged and pounded as if our lives depended on it.

"I'm coming! What is it at this unearthly hour!" Then the gate swung open and a short man in a red great-coat stood there staring at us. He saw the copper and his eyebrows shot up into his hair.

"By hell. Where did you get that? And what's farmer Alan's nags doing tied up to it?"

TEN
The *Alice May*

Well, that's my story told. All you'll need to know is this: We did it.

We had a job getting our money off that dealer, though. First he made out we'd stolen the horses and tried to send us off. Then he tried to fob us off with half a sovereign each for all our work. Davies asked for ten and he started laughing at us. Then he got angry and told us to just cart the copper away and see how far we got. He thought he had us in the palm of his hand.

Davies was in a state . . . wheezing and bubbling and coughing and trying to shout. I thought he was going to pass out on us.

I said, "Listen." I was shaking myself . . . with fear and lust for the money. I said, "We floated this stuff up from the bottom of the river. We spent four days and our friend drowned down there, drowned dead. We did it for one thing . . . to get ourselves a berth on a ship and learn a trade. If you can't pay us enough to get that, you keep the copper and we'll go straight back and tell the ship owners where it is, and that's everyone out of a profit. So you can keep your sovereign. We want enough to buy us our berth, or we'll have nothing at all."

Davies was bent over double, coughing, but I could see him look at me and nod.

The dealer's eyebrows went down to his nose, then back up into his hair. He'd thought we'd do anything for a few coppers, but we'd set our sights high.

He jerked his head. "You better come this way, lads." He took us into the yard, away from the little crowd who had gathered around. Then he put his hands in his pockets and looked down his nose at us.

"Well, my lads," he said softly. "I worked my way up from nothing to own this yard. And I admire what ye've done. So . . . I'll pay you six guineas for it . . . and that's a fair price," he warned when he saw Davies about to complain. "God knows how I'll shift all this copper, stolen and all. But I know what it is to be poor and no way out of it. So long as we understand, I'm only doing this out of the goodness of my heart." And he slipped into our hands six golden guineas.

"Now run home with it, for God's sake, before someone robs you!"

I'd never seen gold before. Neither had Davies. We couldn't believe that so much copper turned into so little gold. But it was money, all right. It was enough money to live on for a year.

We got back to the barge, trying to look like two men who had nothing in the world. The dealer was right . . . there were plenty who'd slit our throats for less. Once we got back we sat and counted it for an hour or so, and weighed it and polished it and put it in and out of our pockets. And then . . . would you believe this? Davies wanted to give Ten Tons his share.

I could feel my heart sink.

"He can't spend it where he is," I said.

"He gets his share, same as us. It's up to him what he does with it," insisted Davies. And you know, he

was ready to take two of those guineas and fling them into the river after Ten Tons. I had the devil's job talking him out of it . . . at least until we'd made sure we had our berths sorted out.

And it was a good job I did. Six guineas is a fortune, but we didn't find it easy getting a master to take us on. We were both scratty little things, and Davies was wheezing away half dead. He didn't look as if he'd make it to the docks, let alone the wide world.

At first we tried to get on the big ships, but they wouldn't touch us. But money works. On Orchard Wharf we found the master of the *Alice May,* an old ketch that plied her way round the coast carrying the big timbers they used for railways, bridges, and the like. Even he looked doubtfully at Davies. But in the end he grinned and shook hands with us.

"Three guineas each, and I'll make seamen of the pair of you!"

So that was it. We had our berths on the *Alice May,* we had our dreams in our pockets! But there was none left over for Ten Tons. And none left over for my family, either.

I felt bad . . . but you don't get such a chance twice. I was so ashamed I never even went to say goodbye, which I regretted as soon as we set sail. But Father would never have let me take all that money away. They wouldn't have understood . . . they'd have called me greedy. Maybe I am, but one day I'll come back and show them what kind of man I've become, and buy them all the good things they never had. This time there wasn't enough to go round, but it won't always be like that.

So for all my bad ways and dreaming ideas, I got work on board ship, which was all I ever wanted. Not much of a boat, but our first place. We got our orders soon enough . . . cleaning and scrubbing and carrying and climbing the ropes. Once we were out of the river the master promised to start teaching us all the things a seaman has to learn. Me and Davies, we're bad lots and no good will come of us, but we did what we set out to do. And the master is a good man, too. He works us hard but he feeds us well. He even let us have a shilling back from our money, to buy flowers for Ten Tons the day we set sail.

We got him a huge bunch of lilies from a flower girl at the rail station. The master goggled when he saw them.

"The whole shilling on flowers!" he groaned. But I think he was impressed, too. He nodded at us and said, "Well, lads, if you show the same loyalty to me as you have to your friend, we'll go far together."

The sail was unfurled. Me and Davies ran to see the anchor go up. The deck hands yelled, "Hove to!" The wind caught the canvas, the deck moved under us. We were away! And I thought . . . no more mud, no more cracking the ice to lever out the coals. Me and Davies, we'd made it. We were our own men now, and in another few hours we'd be out of London and seeing the sea for the first time in our lives.

The ship moved off her moorings and headed out into mid water. It only took a few minutes to get to the place where Ten Tons had drowned. We leaned over and threw our lilies overboard.

"See yer, Tens."

"Good luck, mate!"

The flowers scattered in the wind and floated on the water. It was so sad. They were pretty but there was nothing so good as just being alive. The whole crew went quiet . . . I don't know if it was respect for Ten Tons, or if they were just watching two mad boys throw a shilling away like that.

The *Alice May* pushed on. The lilies bobbed in the water behind us. We were away down to the sea, following after our friend. The only difference was, he was under the water and we were up on top.

GLOSSARY

barmy.   Crazy.

bum.   Backside or rear end.

capstone.   Top of a pillar or wall.

daft.   Silly.

dripping.   Grease left over from cooking meat.

fathom.   A unit of length equal to six feet.

fob off.   To put someone off with something inferior.

gob.   Mouth.

hornpipe.   A lively folk dance.

Paddy-woman.   Slang term for Irishwoman.

pinch.   To steal.

rasher.   Slice of bacon.

scratty.   Dirty and disheveled.

sprities.   Wooden sail support connected to the mast with the sail attached to help it catch the wind.

Ships on the River Thames

barge.   A roomy, usually flat-bottomed boat used chiefly to transport goods on inland waterways and generally propelled by towing.

brig.   A large two-masted **square-rigged ship**; short for *brigantine*.

clipper. General term for a fast sailing ship, especially one with long slender lines, an overhanging bow, tall masts, and a large sail area.

ferry. A boat used to transport passengers, vehicles, or goods; short for *ferry boat*.

ketch. A medium-size two-masted sailboat.

schooner. A large, typically two-masted sailing ship, often with some **square-rigged** sails.

square-rigged ship. A ship on which the mainsails face forward and extend on horizontal crossbeams fastened at their center to the masts.

tall ship. General term for a sailing ship with at least two masts, especially a **square-rigged ship.**

tug. A strongly built, powerful boat used for towing and pushing; short for *tugboat*.

Monetary Units in Victorian England

farthing. 2 farthings = 1 ha'penny.

ha'penny. 2 ha'pence (ha'pennies) = 1 penny.

penny (pl = *pence*). 12 pence = 1 shilling.

shilling. 20 shillings = 1 sovereign.
     21 shillings = 1 guinea.

sovereign. Highest denomination of the time.

guinea. Replaced in 1813 by the sovereign, the term continued to be used for many years.

pound. 1 pound = 1 sovereign.